Text copyright © 2006 by Arlene Hamilton
Illustrations copyright © 2006 by Dean Griffiths

Published in Canada by Fitzhenry & Whiteside,
195 Allstate Parkway, Markham, Ontario L3R 4T8

Published in the United States by Fitzhenry & Whiteside,
311 Washington Street, Brighton, Massachusetts 02135

www.fitzhenry.ca   godwit@fitzhenry.ca

10 9 8 7 6 5 4 3 2 1

Library and Archives Canada Cataloguing in Publication

Hamilton, Arlene, 1950-
Only a cow / Arlene Hamilton ; illustrated by Dean Griffiths.

ISBN-13: 978-1-55041-871-2
ISBN-10: 1-55041-871-8

1. Cows—Juvenile fiction. 2. Domestic animals—Juvenile fiction.
I. Griffiths, Dean, 1967- II. Title.

PS8565.A52O65 2006   jC813'.54   C2006-903248-3

**U.S. Publisher Cataloging-in-Publication Data
(Library of Congress Standards)**

Hamilton, Arlenc, 1950-
Only a cow / Arlene Hamilton ; illustrated by Dean Griffiths.
[32] p. : col. ill. ; cm.
Summary: Lucille isn't like the other cows on Charlie's farm.
She yearns to run in a real race, just like Thunder, Farmer Charlie's prize racehorse.
ISBN-10: 1-55041-871-8
ISBN-13: 978-1-55041-871-2
1. Farm –Fiction – Juvenile literature. 2. Cows – Juvenile fiction.
3. Horses – Juvenile fiction. I. Griffiths, Dean, ill. II. Title.
[E] dc22   PZ10.3H47On 2006

Fitzhenry & Whiteside acknowledges with thanks the Canada Council for the Arts, and the Ontario Arts Council
for their support of our publishing program. We acknowledge the financial support of the Government of Canada
through the Book Publishing Industry Development Program (BPIDP) for our publishing activities.

Design by Wycliffe Smith Design Inc.

Printed in Hong Hong

Only a Cow

BY
ARLENE HAMILTON

ILLUSTRATED BY
DEAN GRIFFITHS

FITZHENRY & WHITESIDE

Charlie Johnson's cows grazed peacefully in their meadow. But as Thunder the racehorse galloped around his field, one head popped up like a periscope. It was Lucille.

She stared at Thunder. His long legs powered him along, and his hoofbeats pounded in her ears. Lucille was spellbound.

Lucille looked back at her friends,
still lazily chewing their cud.

"Bertha," she said, "day in and day out we just stand around in
this same old field. Don't you ever feel like doing something more?"

Bertha looked puzzled. "No," she replied. "This is what cows do."

"Well, we could do something different for a change. Something
exciting."

"Lucille, we're only cows. Cows aren't exciting," said Bertha.

Lucille sighed. She imagined that she was like
Thunder—sleek and powerful, bounding along a racetrack.
"Let's have a race!" she cried. "Come on, girls. Line up!"
The other cows stared at her.

"Are you crazy?" exclaimed Bertha.
"Hey! Stop shoving!" grumbled Ruby.
Josephine sidled away, mumbling something about
heart attacks.

"Hmpff. What do they know?" Lucille muttered, and stomped off.

Thunder cantered over to the fence for a chat. "Just keeping in shape," he said casually. "I have a race at the fairground tomorrow, you know."

"Good luck," said Lucille politely. "I'd like to try life in the fast lane. Have you ever noticed any cows in any of your races?"

"My dear," Thunder said, "horses are horses, and cows are cows. And you are only a cow."

The next morning,
Charlie led Thunder into the
trailer. Then he hurried to the barn.

"County Fair today, ladies," he boomed. "You beauties
are going to win the Cow Show! Come on, now. Step lively."

Lucille and her friends joined Thunder, who calmly
munched his hay. Lucille nudged Bertha aside. She craned her
neck until she could peek out the window.

As the trailer hurtled down the highway, Lucille feasted
her eyes on the sights, while her friends dined on hay.

At the fairground, Charlie blazed a trail through the
bustling crowd. Lucille gawked at all the activity swirling
around her. She stumbled over cables, bumped into people,
and fell farther and farther behind. Just as she realized she
was lost, Lucille heard a bugle blare.

Streams of people were hurrying toward a big stadium,
so Lucille followed them inside.

Behind a long gate in the stadium stood a
row of the most magnificent horses Lucille had ever
seen. On each horse sat a man wearing a brightly
colored uniform.

Lucille squeezed herself into a space between two
of the horses, and looked around.

This must be a race, she thought. Then she heard a
voice she knew.

"Lucille, what are you doing here?" exclaimed
Thunder. "This is a horse race. You're not a horse.
You're only a cow!"

Before Lucille could say a word, a pistol shot blasted her ears. The horses exploded from their stalls.

Lucille froze and gaped at the fleeing horses. As they disappeared around the first bend, a wonderful idea occurred to her.

"Here's my chance!" she cried, and off she charged, clopping and clomping down the track. Her cowbell clattered wildly.

Charlie Johnson sat in the stands cheering Thunder on. His jaw dropped when he spotted a cow—*his* cow—plodding along behind.

"Lucille, what do you think you're doing?" he yelled. "You're not a horse. You're only a cow!"

The spectators began to laugh. Lucille ignored them. "Hmpff. What do they know?" she puffed.

Jogging steadily along the turf, Lucille rounded the first bend. As she plowed into the straightaway, she could hear a distant rumble behind her. It grew louder and louder.

Lucille peeked fearfully over her shoulder. A mass of thundering horses was closing in on her. The ground shook as they pounded past.

Lucille's heart sank. "Why, they've already finished one lap," she panted. But still she forged ahead.

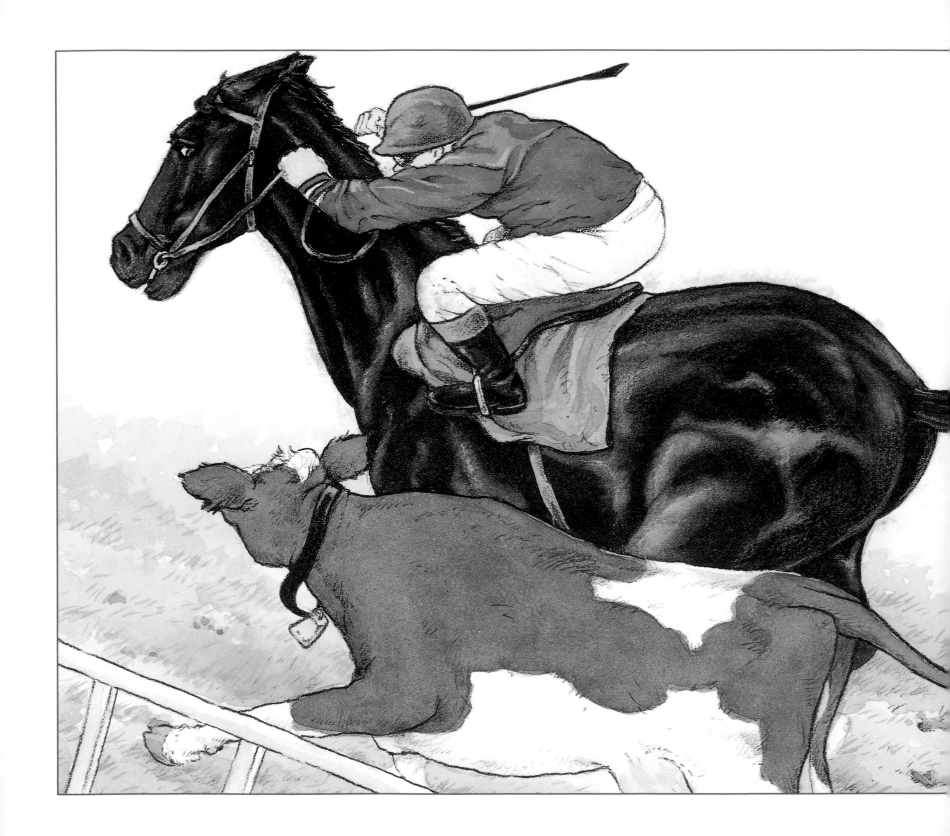

Lucille was almost into the far turn when she heard the same rumble.

"Oh no! Here they come again!" she moaned. Squeezing her eyes shut, Lucille huddled into the railing and waited for the horses to pass.

What on earth am I doing here? she wondered. *Horses are horses, and cows are cows. And I'm only a cow.*

But then, as the horses flew by, Lucille heard Thunder's voice above the pounding.

"Come on, Lucille!" he called.

"Well, I can't let a fellow racer down!" Lucille exclaimed. She squared her shoulders and set out again. "This cow is going to cross that finish line."

Lucille lumbered on and on. At last, she saw the finish line ahead. But it looked so far away. Her hooves were bruised and she was exhausted.

"I didn't know races were this long," she gasped. Her head drooped and she coasted to a walk.

The spectators stopped laughing. Someone shouted, "Come on, girl! Don't give up now!"

Another cried, "Go to it, there, sweetheart! You can do it!"

A boy began yelling, "Go, girl, go! Go, girl, go!" Soon the whole crowd was chanting along with him.

Lucille could hardly believe her ears. She felt as swift and beautiful as a racehorse. And did a racehorse ever quit before the end of a race?

NEVER!

Lucille paid no attention to her aching hooves. She lifted her head grandly and plodded joyously down the home stretch, nodding and mooing to the cheering crowd.

At last she swept jauntily across the finish line.

Charlie proudly led Lucille to the Winner's Circle, where she joined Thunder. The mayor presented her with a special prize ribbon. Photographers crowded around, and Charlie beamed as he posed between his two champions.

Lucille still lives on Charlie's farm. She still
goes out to the same old field, day in and day
out. Sometimes she and Thunder practice their
racing.

And Lucille patiently waits for next year's fair.